DOGGY BUDDIES

Published in the UK by Scholastic Children's Books, 2020
Euston House, 24 Eversholt Street, London, NW1 1DB
A division of Scholastic Limited

London ~ New York ~ Toronto ~ Sydney ~ Auckland
Mexico City ~ New Delhi ~ Hong Kong

SCHOLASTIC and associated logos are trademarks and/or
registered trademarks of Scholastic Inc.

Waffle The Wonder Dog © and TM Darrall Macqueen Ltd 2020
Written by Emily Stead © Scholastic Children's Books

DARRALL
MacQueen LTD

TRADE EDITION ISBN 978 07023 0013 4
SCHOLASTIC CLUBS AND FAIRS EDITION ISBN 978 07023 0073 8

A CIP catalogue record for this book is available from the British Library.

Printed and bound in Italy by L.E.G.O S.p.A

2 4 6 8 10 9 7 5 3 1

www.scholastic.co.uk

Waffle and Evie loved playing together and practising Waffle's amazing tricks. "Waffle, who is my best friend?" Evie asked.

"Me?" woofed Waffle.

"Yes! And who is your best friend?"
asked Evie.

"You!" woofed Waffle again.

Evie loved having Waffle all to herself.

Woof, woof!

In the garden, Simon had set up a
ball pit for Waffle and Evie to play in.
It was so much fun that Simon
decided to play in it too!

Meanwhile, Mrs Hobbs was keeping an eye
on Waffle from over the fence. She was wearing
a hat covered in leaves as a disguise!
"Hello, Mrs Hobbs," said Simon, waving.
But she quickly ducked down again.

"Morning, dog lovers!" came a voice from inside the house. Gramps had arrived!

Evie and Waffle ran into the kitchen.

"Hello, you two cheeky pups!" Gramps smiled. He pulled out a tub from his bag. Inside were three homemade dog biscuits.

"Woof!" barked Waffle, licking his lips. "You'll have to be patient, Waffle, and not gobble your treat straightaway!" Gramps laughed.

"Aww!" woofed Waffle sadly.

Gramps had invited two more dogs round to play. Waffle would have to wait until the play date to share the doggy treats.

"You're going to love Trevor and Violet, Waffle," said Gramps.

"Woof!" barked Waffle.

"Can I still play with you too, Waffle?" said Evie in a worried voice.

But before Waffle could reply, the doorbell rang. *Ding-dong!*

Two dogs raced into the house with their owner, Mr Willow.

The pups looked just like Waffle!

"We couldn't wait to meet wonderful Waffle," smiled Mr Willow.

Trevor and Violet were very excited — they could smell the dog biscuits! The pups jumped up at Gramps and wagged their tails.

"No, no, no!" said Waffle. "Good doggies do this!"

Trevor and Violet watched as Waffle stayed sitting nicely, waiting for his biscuit. Then they did the same.

Mr Willow was amazed — he had never met a dog as clever as Waffle before!

"Well done, Waffle," said Gramps. "I think the pups deserve their biscuits now." And he handed each pup a treat.

Next, everyone went outside to play in the garden.

Waffle was excited to play with his new friends, and the pups were running around all over the place!

Evie wanted to show Gramps and Mr Willow Waffle's new tricks. But when she called for Waffle, he didn't come. Evie frowned.

"Don't worry, Evie," smiled Gramps. "Waffle is just excited to play with Trevor and Violet. We can show Mr Willow what Waffle can do later."
Evie felt sad. Waffle was too busy playing with his new friends to notice her.

Evie went inside for some peace and quiet.
She looked out of her bedroom window.
Everybody was having fun without her.

"Waffle has some new best friends now," Evie sighed to her teddies.

The next minute, though, Waffle came bounding up the stairs to see her.

"Waffle!" smiled Evie. "I was missing you."

"Me too," Waffle woofed. "So let's go outside and play together, pleeease!" he begged.

Evie smiled.

Suddenly, Mrs Hobbs's dog alarm started going off. *Woo-woo! Woo-woo! Woo-woo!*

When Evie looked out of the window, she saw that one of the pups had got into Mrs Hobbs's garden! "Oh no!" cried Evie.

Waffle and Evie hurried downstairs to help.

Trevor chased Violet, and then Waffle followed next door too!

"I thought we'd fixed that hole in the fence!" said Simon as he and Evie peered through the hole into Mrs Hobbs' garden.

"Please could you turn the alarm off?" Jess shouted over the noise to Mrs Hobbs.

But Mrs Hobbs was furious! "There are three dogs in my garden," she said crossly. "George has run inside, scared."

Mr Willow tried to help. He crawled through the fence and shouted, "Violet, Trevor! Come here, at once!"

But the cheeky pups didn't listen!
They were busy trying to find George the cat.

It was time for Waffle to take charge. "Violet, Trevor! Stop!" he woofed. "George the cat is my friend. Go back through the fence so he can come out and play."

This time, to everyone's surprise, Trevor and Violet did exactly what they were told.

"Will you look at that!" gasped Mr Willow. "What a Wonder Dog Waffle is!"

With Trevor and Violet safely back in the Brooklyn-Bells' garden, George came out to thank Waffle.

"Don't worry, Georgey," woofed Waffle, giving the cat a friendly lick. "They've gone."

"Miaow!" said George.

"How sweet," smiled Jess. "A dog and a cat that want to be friends!" Waffle tried to make friends with Mrs Hobbs too, but she wasn't quite so friendly ... instead of giving him a cuddle, Mrs Hobbs switched on the noisy dog alarm again!

What a busy day it had been! It was finally time to read Waffle's bedtime story.

"Ready, Waffle?" asked Jess.

"Woof!" barked Waffle, snuggling down between Simon and Jess.

Jess turned to the first page. "This is the story of a soppy, silly dog called Waffle..." she began.

Waffle was very tired after a busy day and he quickly fell fast asleep.

Good night, Waffle!